Dear Junior Gymnast:

I'm Dominique Dawes, and gymnastics is my favorite sport! But it takes a lot of work to be a great gymnast. When I was training for the Olympics, I spent five to eight hours a day practicing with my coach. I even trained on Saturdays!

Lots of people ask me if it's hard to spend six days a week workng out. But I don't think so—I think it's fun! I love tumbling, and I have a lot of friends at the gym. It's my favorite place to be.

But I do need <u>some</u> time off! Every Sunday, I spend the day with my family or with friends from school. I don't even <u>think</u> about gymnastics! And when I get back to the gym on Monday, I'm relaxed and ready to tumble!

In this book, Amanda Calloway wants to be an Olympic hopeful. But will she give up her family and friends in order to be a perfect 10?

Keep reading!

*Dominique Dawes*

# Read more books about the Junior Gymnasts!

# Amanda's Perfect 10

# JUNIOR GYMNASTS

## Amanda's Perfect 10

### BY TEDDY SLATER

illustrated by Wayne Alfano

A
**LITTLE APPLE**
PAPERBACK

SCHOLASTIC INC.
New York Toronto London Auckland Sydney

With special thanks to
Tom Manganiello of the
57th Street Magic Gym.

A PARACHUTE PRESS BOOK

ISBN 0-590-85999-4

Text copyright © 1996 by Parachute Press, Inc.
Illustrations copyright © 1996 by Scholastic Inc.
Inside cover photo © Doug Pensinger/ALLSPORT USA.
LITTLE APPLE PAPERBACKS and the LITTLE APPLE PAPERBACKS logo
are trademarks of Scholastic Inc.

12 11 10 9 8 7 6 5 4 3 2 1          6 7 8 9/9 0 1/0

Printed in the U.S.A.                                    40

First Scholastic printing, August 1996

*For the girls on my team —*
*Laura, Susan, Heather, Jane, and Joan*

# Contents

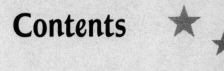

# The Visitor

"And now," Coach Jody announced, "our last performer of the day — Amanda Calloway! Amanda is the newest member of our Level 5 team. She's nine years old, and she's been doing gymnastics for almost six years!"

Everyone in the audience clapped as I marched to the uneven parallel bars. Coach Jody's teaching assistant, Buddy, was waiting there to spot me.

"Are you ready, Amanda?" he asked.

I looked up at the uneven bars. Then I looked out at the audience. I saw my mom

1

and dad, my two sisters, my brother, and my grandmother. They took up the whole first row! I blew them a kiss.

"I'm ready," I told Buddy.

Today was Visitors' Day at Jody's Gym. The gymnasts in my class were putting on a special program for our families and friends.

I tugged at my lucky yellow leotard and took a deep breath. Buddy moved closer to the bars. A spotter has to be ready to catch the gymnast in case she falls.

But I knew I wouldn't fall. I hardly ever do. Besides, today was Thursday — my lucky day!

I grabbed onto the low bar and went right into a front hip circle. Then I swung onto the high bar. The rest of my routine seemed to fly by. *I* was flying!

After my dismount, I turned to where my family was sitting. But they weren't sitting anymore. They were on their feet, yelling "Bravo!" So were some people who *weren't* related to me!

I glanced over at Coach Jody. I thought she would be proud that I had done such a great routine. Coach Jody wasn't even watching me! She was busy talking to a tall, blond man. But he wasn't as tall as Coach Jody — she's over six feet!

Everyone kept clapping while I walked back to the bench. All my friends from class were there — Katie Magee, Dana Lewis, Liz Halsey, Emily Stone, and Hannah Rose Crenshaw. They had already done their routines.

Katie jumped up and hugged me. "Yay, Amanda!" she cried.

Katie is my very best friend in Springfield. When I first moved here from Chicago, she was my *only* friend. Now Dana and I are friends, too.

Katie, Dana, and I don't look anything

alike. Katie has long blond hair and green eyes. Dana has curly red hair and blue eyes. I have dark brown hair and brown eyes. But we all have one big thing in common. We're crazy about gymnastics!

As Coach Jody walked to the front of the gym, Dana scooted over on the bench. Katie and I sat down next to her.

"That ends the Visitors' Day program," Coach Jody announced. "Before we say good-bye, let's give our whole team a hand."

All the visitors clapped again. So did the tall, blond man.

I poked Dana in the side. "Did you see Coach Jody talking to that guy?" I whispered. "She didn't even watch my routine! Do you think he's her boyfriend?"

"You're kidding!" Dana whispered back. "Don't you know who that is?"

"It's Jon Sokolov!" Katie exclaimed. "The famous gymnastics coach!" It's a good thing the audience was still clapping, because she was practically screaming.

I took another look at the tall man.

"Oh, wow!" I said. "It really is Jon Sokolov! What is *he* doing here?"

"Maybe he's searching for new students," Dana said.

Katie gasped. "That must be it! He travels around looking for talented gymnasts, and then he takes them to his gym in Texas. Half the girls on the last Olympic team trained there."

I turned to look at Jon Sokolov again, but I couldn't see him. The gym was crowded with visitors on their way out the doors. When the last one was gone, Coach Jody came over to us. And Jon Sokolov was right behind her! "Congratulations, girls!" Coach Jody said. "You all did great!"

Then she smiled. "In case you didn't notice, we had an extra-special visitor today. Say hello to Coach Jon Sokolov!"

"Hello, Coach Sokolov!" I called. Everyone else just giggled.

"That's it for today," Coach Jody said. "I'll see you all on Monday."

As I headed for the locker room, Coach Jody patted me on the back. "Good routine, kiddo!" she said.

I looked up at Coach Jody. Then I looked up at Jon Sokolov. They were both so tall it made me dizzy.

"Ah, the lady in yellow," Jon Sokolov said. "And what is your name?" he asked me.

"Amanda," I told him. "Amanda Calloway."

"Well, Amanda Calloway," Jon Sokolov said. "That was some routine you just did. In fact, it was almost a perfect ten. If only you'd kept your toes pointed on the dismount."

I was so excited I could hardly speak.

"Th-thank you, Mr. Sokolov," I finally blurted out.

"You're very welcome," he said. "But watch those toes. I'll be back next week, and I want to see some progress!"

"I'm sure you will," Coach Jody told him. "Amanda is a very hard worker. She gets better every day."

She gave my ponytail a gentle tug and said, "Go shower before your muscles tighten up."

"Okay," I said. "Bye, Coach Jody. Good-bye, Mr. Sokolov."

My friends were all waiting for me in the locker room. The minute I walked in, they rushed over.

"What did he say?" Katie asked.

"What did he want?" Dana demanded.

"I don't know," I answered. "First he asked me what my name was. Then he said I was an almost perfect ten."

"Jon Sokolov called you a perfect ten!" Katie screeched.

*"Almost,"* I repeated. "He told me to point my toes."

"Is that all?" Hannah Rose asked.

"No," I said. "He said he would be back next week to see if I'm a perfect ten."

"Oh, my gosh!" Katie squealed. "I can't believe it! You've been discovered by Jon Sokolov! You have an audition with a real Olympic coach!"

"Wait a minute, Katie!" I said. "He didn't say anything about an audition."

"But that must be what he meant," Dana said. "Why else would he be coming back to see you?"

"Dana is right!" Katie cried. She was jumping up and down with excitement.

"Of course I am," Dana said. "This is exactly what happened to Suzanne Dillon when she trained here. Jon Sokolov auditioned her, and she moved down to Texas. Now she lives there and trains there and everything. Maybe he'll want *you* to go there, Amanda."

"I still don't think he meant that," I said.

"He did!" Katie insisted.

"Do you really think so?" I asked.

"Really!" Dana said.

"Really!" Katie yelled.

"REALLY!" everyone screamed together.

They couldn't all be wrong.

I grinned. Wow! *Me*, auditioning for Jon Sokolov!

# The Big Secret

"Mandy! Gretch! Gab! Pete! Gran! J.J.!" my mother called. "Dinner's ready!"

Mom never calls anyone by their whole name. With so many people in our family, I guess it saves time.

Mandy is short for Amanda. Gretch is my big sister Gretchen. Gab is my little sister Gabriella. Pete is my big brother Peter. Gran is our granny. And J.J.'s our dad — James Jefferson Calloway.

There are lots of people in our house. But that's not all! We have the same number of pets as people. Seven! Tuna the cat, Zelda

11

the dog, Farfel the ferret, Polly and Golly the parrots, and Hoppy and Happy the rabbits. Mom calls them Tune, Zell, Farf, Pee & Gee, and The Buns — short for bunnies!

"Did anyone feed the animals?" Dad asked as we headed for the dining room. They always get fed before we do. Otherwise they beg like crazy.

"It's Amanda's turn," Gabby said, plopping down next to me. "I did it yesterday."

"And I did it the day before," Peter said. "It's Aman — "

"Well, I think Amanda deserves a rest after her magnificent performance this afternoon," Dad broke in.

"Amanda," he said, patting me on the head. "I hereby declare you chore-less tonight!" Then he stood up and bowed to me. "I would be honored to feed our furry friends for you."

I giggled. "Thanks, Daddy," I said.

"Polly and Golly aren't furry," Gabby

pointed out. "They're feathery." But Daddy was already in the pantry, scooping out kibble, seeds, and bunny bits. We have a whole cabinet just for pet food.

"Seriously," Dad said when he came back to the table. "You were definitely the star of Visitors' Day, Amanda. I was very proud of you."

I knew he'd be even prouder when he heard about my audition with a famous coach. But before I could tell him, Gabby announced that her ballet class was having a recital. Then Peter started talking about his high school basketball team. Gretchen rolled her eyes. She goes to high school, too, but she thinks basketball is dumb.

I was about to interrupt my brother when Granny began talking. No one ever interrupts her.

Oh, well, I thought. Maybe it would be better to wait until *after* I passed the audition. Then it would be *really* big news. So for the rest of the meal I didn't say a word. I just sat there and imagined myself training with Mr. Sokolov in Texas.

After dinner, I went upstairs to my room. I was on my second math problem when the phone rang. It was Katie.

"Hi, Katie," I said. "What's up?"

"I found this great book in the library," she said. "It's called *The Winning Way!* and it's all about training for the Olympics. There's a whole chapter on Mary Lou Retton."

"Wow!" I said. Mary Lou Retton is my idol! Everyone in my gymnastics class wants to be just like her. I wasn't even born when Mary Lou won the 1984 Olympics, but I've seen all her routines on video.

"Listen to this," Katie said. "It says Mary Lou practiced eight hours a day to get ready for the Olympics. She got up at five-thirty every morning! Her whole training schedule is printed here in the book."

"Wow!" I said again. "Can I borrow it?"

"Of course!" Katie laughed. "I got it for you! You can follow Mary Lou's schedule to get ready for your audition. I'll bring it to school tomorrow."

"Thanks," I said. "I can't wait to read it. See you in the morning."

As soon as we said good-bye, I picked up my alarm clock and set it for 5:30. Then I laid out my clothes for the next day.

Friday is my green day. I have a different lucky color for every day of the week. I hung my green leotard and warm-up suit over my desk chair. My green hightops went underneath the chair. Then I went into my closet and pulled down a dark-green corduroy jumper and a mint-green sweater.

When I came out of the closet, Gabby and Zelda were standing in front of the ballet barre on my wall. Dad bought the barre when I was taking ballet lessons. I stopped ballet two years ago, but I still use the barre to stretch out and warm up for gymnastics.

Gabby was trying to lift her right leg onto the barre. "This is too high," she complained.

"No it's not," I said. "You're just too low!" Gabby's only six, and she's kind of small for her age.

Zelda licked Gabby's foot. Then she rested her nose on the barre. Zelda isn't even a year old yet, but she's already taller than Gabby! Zelda is a Great Dane.

Gabby wiped her wet toes on my rug. Then she twirled across the room and plopped down on my bed.

"Will you help me practice for my ballet recital?" she asked. "I get to be an autumn leaf! My teacher says I have to blow in the wind."

Gabby bounced up off the bed and

began waving her arms up and down. "This is when the leaves fall off the tree," she said. "Want to see the rest?"

"Not now, Gab," I told her. "I have a lot to do tonight. In fact, I'm going to be really busy all week."

"Doing what?" Gabby asked.

"It's a secret," I whispered.

"I can keep a secret," Gabby said.

"Uh-uh," I said. "I'll tell you next week."

"Tell me now," Gabby whined. "Please, please, please, please, please, please, please, plea — "

"All right, all right!" I finally gave in. "But you have to promise not to tell Mommy and Daddy. I want to surprise them."

"I promise," Gabby said.

"Okay," I said. "I can't help you practice for your recital because I have to practice for my gymnastics audition with Jon

Sokolov. I only have one week to become a perfect ten!"

"Oh," Gabby said. She waved her arms some more. "What's an audition?" she asked. "And who's Jon Socklove?"

"An audition is when you try out for something — like a play," I explained.

Gabby nodded.

"And it's Jon *Sokolov*," I added. "Not Socklove. He's the most famous gymnastics coach in the world. And if he thinks I'm good enough, he'll let me move to Texas and train with him."

"You're *moving*?" Gabby exclaimed. "To *Texas*?"

"Uh-huh," I said. "Lots of Olympic gymnasts train there! Isn't that exciting?"

"Yeah," Gabby said. But she didn't sound excited. She sounded kind of sad. "Isn't Texas far away?"

"It's not *that* far," I said.

"Can I visit?" Gabby asked.

"Sure," I told her. "At least, I think I can have visitors." I thought for a minute. "I'm not really sure how Mr. Sokolov's gym works," I said. "The girls there train for hours and hours every day. They might be too busy for visitors."

Gabby frowned. And suddenly I felt sad, too. I wanted to train with Jon Sokolov, and I really wanted to be in the Olympics. But I wasn't so sure about the Texas part. I was just beginning to feel at home here in Springfield. Did I really want to move *again*?

# 3

# Me And Mary Lou

I got up at 5:30 on Friday morning. Just like Mary Lou Retton! It was still dark outside, but I hopped right out of bed. If I wanted to be a perfect ten by the time Jon Sokolov came back, I had no time to waste.

I did some stretches at the barre. As soon as my muscles felt loose, I put on my green warm-up suit. Then I tiptoed downstairs, through the kitchen, and into the backyard.

The sun wasn't up yet, and it was freezing out. I warmed up with fifty jumping jacks, fifty leg lifts, and fifty sit-ups. Then

I stepped onto the mini balance beam my brother made for me.

The mini beam is much lower than a regular beam, so it's great for practicing. You don't have to worry about falling off.

I did my whole beam routine a few times. Mr. Sokolov would have been proud of my pointed toes! Then I did some swing turns. I did ten in a row with my toes super-pointed. While I was doing the turns, I counted "One toe, two toes, three toes . . ." to keep focused.

I tried the same thing with my hand-stands. But just as I said, "Eight toes," I fell off the beam. I had to start from one again. This time I got all the way to ten.

I was working on my cartwheels when I heard someone call:

"Mandy! *Man*-dy!"

Mom stood at the back door in her robe and slippers. "What in the world are

you doing out here in the cold?" she hollered.

But before I could answer, she said, "Go get ready for school. We're having blueberry pancakes for breakfast!"

"Yum!" I said. "I'm starving."

An hour later, Katie rode up our driveway. She only lives a block away, so she always bikes to school with Gabby and me. We all go to Washington Elementary. I'm in fourth grade. Katie is in third grade, and Gabby is in first.

By the time we got to school, I was totally tired. And it wasn't even eight o'clock yet!

Katie reached into her bike basket. "Here's that book I told you about," she said. "*The Winning Way!* It's got everything you need to know about training for the Olympics."

"Amanda isn't in the Olympics *yet!*" Gabby said.

Katie smiled at her. "But she might be, if she passes the audition with Jon Sokolov."

"Keep your fingers crossed!" I said. I crossed my fingers and kept them crossed till I got to my classroom.

I love school. And I really love my teacher, Ms. Cooper. But today I couldn't wait for school to end. All I wanted to do was go home and practice gymnastics.

After lunch, Ms. Cooper said, "We're going to review the state capitals."

Ugh! I thought. Capitals are *so* boring! But the minute Ms. Cooper turned toward the big map on the blackboard, I got a great idea. I took out my notebook. Then I took out *The Winning Way!* and slipped it between the pages of the notebook.

While everyone else copied down capitals, I read about Mary Lou Retton. It was a million times more interesting!

I was just at the part where Mary Lou meets Coach Karolyi when a big hand reached down and snatched up Katie's book.

"I'll hold onto this for now," Ms. Cooper said sternly. "And I'll see *you* after school, Amanda!"

At three o'clock, all the other kids ran out of the room. In a minute, no one was left but me.

And Ms. Cooper.

Ms. Cooper motioned me up to her desk. "Amanda," she said. "I'm very disappointed in you. Not only did you miss an important lesson, but you were very rude to me."

"I'm sorry, Ms. Cooper," I said. "I didn't think of it that way. I would never be rude on purpose."

"I'm sure you wouldn't," she said.

"You're a very polite young lady. Apology accepted," she added with a smile.

"Thanks!" I smiled, too.

"Of course, that still leaves the matter of the lesson you missed," Ms. Cooper went on.

I stopped smiling.

"I have some paperwork to do in the office," Ms. Cooper said. "I want you to spend that time here, writing down all the state capitals. At four o'clock I'll come back and give you your gymnastics book and you can give me my state capitals. Do we have a deal?" she asked.

"Deal!" I said.

As soon as Ms. Cooper left the room, I started writing down capitals. I didn't even peek at the map. I know them all.

It was only 3:15 when I finished. I stared at the clock for a while. It felt like an hour had gone by. But it was only 3:20!

I got up from my desk and walked

around the room. That made me feel better, so I walked a little faster. Then I started jogging. After three laps, I checked the clock again. 3:25.

More than a half hour until I could go home and practice! I shouldn't waste time, I told myself. I pushed all the desks to one side of the room. Then I took off my green hightops and did my floor exercise!

The next time I looked at the clock, it was almost 4:00! I shoved the desks back where they belonged, put on my sneakers, and waited for Ms. Cooper.

"Hi, Mommy," I called. "Sorry I'm late. I was — "

"I know where you were, Amanda," my mother said. "Ms. Cooper called and told me all about it." I could tell she was mad. That's the only time Mom ever uses my whole name.

"I'm sorry," I told her. "Really I am."

"Listen, Amanda," Mom said. "I know how much you care about gymnastics. But school is important, too. You can't neglect one for the other."

"I know," I said. "It won't happen again. I promise!"

"Good girl," Mom answered. "That's all I need to hear." She hugged me tight. "Now, it's getting late. Would you please go get Gabby from Katie's house? I don't want her out alone after dark."

"Katie's?" I exclaimed. "What's Gabby doing there?"

"Practicing for her ballet recital," Mom said. "You haven't forgotten about it, have you?"

"Of course not," I said. "What kind of a big sister do you think I am?"

"A wonderful one," my mother said, giving me another hug. "And I'm sure Gabby thinks so, too."

"I hope so," I said. But all of a sudden,

I wasn't so sure! The truth is, I *had* forgotten about Gabby's ballet recital. All I could think of was my own audition!

I climbed on my bike and pedaled toward Katie's house. At least Katie was around to help Gabby, I thought. But I shouldn't have forgotten about the recital.

A good big sister would have remembered.

# 4

# Gold Medal Meals

*BRRRIIING!*

Saturday morning the alarm clock rang at 5:30. But I was too tired to get up. I turned it off and went back to sleep.

*PIIING!* The next thing I knew it was 7:45. Something was rattling against my window.

*PIIING!* There it was again. It sounded like a hailstorm.

I got up and looked outside. Katie and Dana stood on my lawn, tossing pebbles up at the glass. When they ran out of rocks, I raised the window.

"Shhh!" I hissed. "You'll wake my folks!" I shut the window, put a sweatshirt over my nightgown, and ran downstairs.

My friends were waiting at the back door. "What are you doing here so early?" I asked. "You woke me up."

"We came to make you breakfast!" Katie said.

"But if you're going to be so grouchy," Dana added, "we'll just go away."

"No we won't," Katie said, marching into the house.

Dana looked at me and shrugged. Then she followed Katie.

I felt kind of silly standing in the hallway alone. So I followed them into the kitchen.

Katie was dumping the stuff from her backpack onto the counter when Gabby came downstairs.

"What's going on?" Gabby asked, picking up Katie's pencil case.

"Keep your hands to yourself," I told Gabby. She always has to touch everything.

"Katie doesn't care if I play with it," Gabby said. But she put the pencil case down.

"What *is* going on?" I asked Katie.

Katie reached into her bag and pulled out a book.

I looked at the cover. *"Gold Medal Meals,"* I read out loud.

"Uh-huh," Katie said. "It's full of power-food recipes from all the great Olympic champs."

I turned to the table of contents. "Tofu Supreme . . . Cauliflower Casserole . . . Liquid Liver!"

*"Liquid liver?"* Gabby made a gagging sound.

"Yuck!" I said. "That sounds disgusting."

"And hard to make," Dana said.

Katie picked up the book and flipped

33

through the pages. "Here's an easy one," she said. "A Banana Bubbly! You make it in the blender. And it only has four ingredients."

"Let me see," I said, peering over her shoulder. "What's in it?"

The book dropped out of Katie's hands and fell on the floor with a crash. As Katie bent down to get it, her long blond hair fell over her face. "Yogurt, bananas, and ice cubes," she said.

"That's only three ingredients," I said. "What's the fourth one?"

"Uh . . . reggs," Katie mumbled through her hair.

"Uhreggs?" I repeated. "What are uhreggs?"

"Ruh-*eggs*! she said a little louder. She was still bending down, only now she was tying her shoelace.

"I think she said raw eggs," Gabby piped up.

"Raw eggs!" I yelped. "Gross! I don't

care *how* healthy they are. I am *not* eating any raw eggs!"

"Okay," Katie said, standing up again. "How about just the yogurt, ice, and banana?"

"I hate yogurt!" I said.

"Don't be so picky," Dana told me. "If you want to perform like a perfect ten, you have to eat like one."

"Oh, all right," I said. "But it better not be *too* gross."

"That's the spirit!" Katie cried. Before I could change my mind, she took two ripe bananas out of the fruit bowl.

Dana opened the refrigerator and began moving stuff around. "I don't see any yogurt," she said after a while.

"How about sour cream?" Katie asked, shoving her head into the fridge. "That's sort of the same."

"Cottage cheese is healthier," Dana said, grabbing a container.

"Cottage cheese is disgusting!" I said. But Dana was already scooping big white globs of it into the blender.

Katie peeled a banana and tossed it in. Then she added some ice cubes and pushed the Whip button.

*WHOOSH! WHIRR!* It was all mooshed together.

Katie poured a big glassful. "Mmm!" she said. "This looks great. Just like a milk-shake!"

Dana put her nose right into the glass. "Smells great, too," she said. "Like banana cream pie."

"Come on, Amanda," Gabby urged. "Try it."

"Yeah, try it!" Katie and Dana said together.

*"Try it! Try it!"* screeched Polly and Golly.

I tried it.

"YECH! BLECH!" I spat it out on the floor. "That's the grossest thing I ever tasted!"

Zelda galloped in from nowhere and licked up the mess.

"It can't be that bad," Dana said. "Your *dog* likes it."

"Zelda likes chicken guts!" I yelled. "What does *she* know?"

I ran over to the sink and got a glass of water. I drank it all in one gulp to wash the gross taste out of my mouth. My friends just watched me.

"If you don't mind," I said, "I'm going to have a normal breakfast!" I poured some Fruit Tooties and milk into a bowl and sat down at the table.

Katie picked up the cereal box and read the label. "Hey, this is healthy, too," she said. "It has lots of vitamins." She filled a bowl for herself, one for Dana, and one for Gabby.

For a while we all sat there munching Fruit Tooties. Gabby finished first. She eats even faster than Zelda.

As soon as she slurped the last drop of milk from the bottom of the bowl, Gabby jumped up from the table. "Wait here," she said. "I'll be right back."

The rest of us were still eating when Gabby returned. She held a one-armed brown bear in one hand and a matching brown bear arm in the other.

"Can you sew Bubba back together?" she asked, plopping the bear parts onto the table.

"Sorry, Gab," I said. "Not now. You know I have to get ready for my audition. But I promise I'll do anything you want the minute it's over."

"When will that be?" Gabby demanded.

"I already told you. Next week."

"But *when* next week?" she whined.

I hate it when Gabby whines. But before I could tell her to stop, a horrible thought popped into my head.

"Oh, my gosh!" I cried. "I don't *know*! Mr. Sokolov just said next week. He didn't say what day!"

"Well, he said it last Thursday," Katie said. "So he probably meant *next* Thursday."

"I hope so!" I said. "Thursday is my lucky day."

"You know, it *could* be Wednesday," Dana pointed out. "Or even Monday. Next week could mean anything."

"But it has to be Thursday!" I cried. "Monday is too soon. I won't have time to practice. And Wednesday is my *least* lucky day. I never do anything right on Wednesdays!"

"A-*man*-da!" Dana groaned. "That is *so* superstitious!"

"Don't worry, Amanda," Katie said. "You're a super gymnast. You'll do fine no matter when Jon Sokolov shows up."

"Right," I said. "As long as it's Thursday!"

# 5
# Sneaky Saturday

"This is bad!" Katie said. "*Really* bad! I can't believe I let you guys talk me into this."

It was one o'clock that afternoon, and Katie, Dana, and I were standing outside Coach Jody's office. Katie's face was bright pink and her hands were shaking. "We can't sneak into Coach Jody's office!" she insisted.

"Oh, Katie," Dana said. "Don't be such a worrywart. It's no big deal."

"I am not a worrywart!" Katie argued. "Am I?" she asked worriedly.

"Shhh!" Dana hissed. "Someone will hear you."

"Oh, my gosh!" Katie shrieked. Then she clapped a hand over her mouth.

I looked up and down the corridor. Jody's Gym was practically empty. Saturdays are always pretty quiet. There are no team workouts — only beginner classes.

"Calm down, Katie," Dana said. "No one will hear us. And we're not doing anything wrong anyway. If Coach Jody's office is locked, we'll go right home again."

"And if it's open," I said, "we'll just peek at her desk and find out when Jon Sokolov is coming. *Then* we'll go home!"

"Why can't you just *ask* Coach Jody?" Katie whispered.

"Because she's never here on Saturdays," I explained. "And if I wait till Monday, it may be too late."

I took a step toward Coach Jody's door.

Katie grabbed my sleeve. "Wait!" she cried. "What if someone sees us?"

"They won't," Dana said. "Coach Jody is at the Level 7 meet in Riverdale. And Buddy's in the gym with the little kids."

"Well, if you say so . . ." Katie still looked nervous.

"Listen, Katie," I said. "If you don't want to do it, you don't have to. Dana and I will go in alone."

"Good idea," Dana said. "Katie can wait out here and be our lookout."

"I can?" Katie asked. Her hands stopped shaking.

"Yup," I said. "Make a noise if anybody comes."

I put my hand on the doorknob. But before I could turn it, the office door swung open.

Katie jumped a mile. I thought she was going to have a heart attack. Even Dana and I jumped. Then we all giggled.

Dana stepped inside. "Relax," she said. "There's no one here."

I followed Dana into the office and shut the door behind us. Coach Jody's office was tiny! My walk-in closet at home is bigger.

"Wow!" I said. "What a mess." I could hardly see Coach Jody's desk. There were about a million books and papers piled up there. The floor was just as bad.

"Let's look on her desk first," I suggested. "She must have an appointment calendar. My mom says all grown-ups do."

"Hey, look at this!" Dana said. She pointed to a carton marked ELITE UNIFORMS. "I want to see those."

"Dana," I said. "We have to find the calendar."

But Dana was already opening the box.

"Isn't this beautiful?" she exclaimed, pulling out a bright blue leotard with shiny gold stars around the neck. "I wonder if *we'll* ever be on the Elite team."

"Of course we will," I said.

The Elite gymnasts are the very best. They're the ones who compete at all the big national and international meets.

I took the leotard from Dana and put it back in the box. Then I picked up a big stack of papers from the desk. Suddenly I heard footsteps out in the hallway. I turned toward the door. The knob was turning!

Dana screamed.

I dropped the whole batch of papers.

Coach Jody is back! I thought. We're dead!

But it was only Katie.

"Katie!" I gasped. "You scared us to death! What are you doing in here?"

"It was t-t-too scary outside," Katie whispered. "I was afraid someone would come."

Dana rolled her eyes. "That's the

whole point of a lookout," she told Katie. "To warn us if someone comes."

Katie tiptoed across the room. "I know," she said, still in a whisper. "Sorry."

"Katie, stop whispering," I said. "You're making me nervous."

"And you don't have to tiptoe either," Dana said. "The floor is carpeted."

"Sorry," Katie apologized again. "Maybe I should go back outside."

"No," Dana said. "Stay! We need you to help us."

"Okay," Katie said. She plopped down on the floor and began picking up the papers I had dropped.

Meanwhile, Dana went over to the desk. "Check this out," she said, handing me a framed photo of our coach. Coach Jody looked much younger — and shorter. She was wearing a gold medal around her neck and hugging two girls who looked just like her.

"Do you think those are her sisters?" Dana asked.

"I don't know," I said. "But you'd better put that back where you found it. We're supposed to be looking for Coach Jody's calendar, not just snooping around."

Just then Katie said, "Hey! I think I found something!" She held up a pink slip of paper.

"What is it?" I asked.

"It's a phone message," Katie answered. "It says: *Jon S., Farmer B's, noon, Wed.*"

"Oh, no," I cried. " 'Wed.' must mean Wednesday. Jon Sokolov is coming on my most unlucky day! What am I going to do?"

"Wait a minute," Katie said. "Here's another slip. This one says: *J.S., gm, 4:30 Thurs.*"

"Let me see," I said, grabbing both papers from her hand. "I don't understand. Wednesday . . . Thursday? Which is it?"

"I bet it's both!" Dana said. "Farmer B's

is that new restaurant around the corner. And 'gm' *has* to be gym!"

Katie and I stared at Dana. "So?" I asked.

"*So*, they're probably going out to lunch on Wednesday to talk about you," Dana explained. "And then he's coming here the next day for your audition."

"Thursday!" Katie exclaimed. "Your lucky day!"

"All *riiight*!" I said. "That gives us four days to get me ready for it. Four and a half if we count tonight."

I took the pile of papers from Katie and put them back on Coach Jody's desk.

"Let's get out of here," I said. "I have to go home and practice!"

# 6
# Coach Katie

Tuesday after school, Katie, Gabby, and I met at the bike rack the way we always do.

"Let's go over to Dana's," Katie suggested. "You can use her trampoline to work on your vaults."

"Sure," I agreed. Our team doesn't meet on Tuesdays. But I still had to practice. My audition was only two days away!

"Wait," Katie said as I pulled my bicycle from the rack. "I have an idea. Why don't you leave your bike here! Jogging is much better exercise. Gabby and I can ride next to you."

51

"Great!" I said, dropping my backpack into Katie's basket. "By the time we get to Dana's I'll be all warmed up."

I started to jog. Katie and Gabby pedaled along next to me.

"Did you ever see *The Nutcracker*?" Gabby asked.

"You know I did," I said. "We saw it together last Christmas."

"Not *you*," Gabby said. "I'm talking to Katie."

Katie grinned. "*The Nutcracker* is my favorite ballet," she told Gabby.

"Someday I want to be a Sugarplum Fairy," Gabby went on. "But now I'm only a leaf. Wait till you see my recital costume, Katie! It has sparkly gold things all over the front."

I tuned out Gabby's voice. She didn't want to talk to me, anyway. Instead, I looked at the trees and houses as I jogged. Even though Springfield was really different from

Chicago, it was starting to feel like home. I had made friends here. I loved my new school, my new house, my new gym. Especially my new gym — and Coach Jody!

"Hey, Katie," I said. "I wonder what Coach Sokolov is like. I bet he's strict."

Katie didn't answer. I looked around. She and Gabby were already a block ahead of me. "Hey, guys! Slow down!" I yelled.

Katie turned around and giggled. "Oops," she said, riding back to me. "I guess we were so busy talking that we forgot you were running!"

Gabby laughed.

"I think maybe I'm too young to go to Texas," I told Katie. "Maybe I should stay here with Coach Jody a little longer."

"No way!" Katie cried. "This is your big chance! Anyway, Mr. Sokolov trains girls even younger than you. You have to go!"

"But I'll miss everybody," I protested.

"We'll write to you," Katie said.

"Just what you need," I said. "Another pen pal." Katie already has fourteen pen pals in eleven different countries.

"You can be my fifteenth!" Katie said. She sounded so excited. Like she couldn't wait for me to leave.

I didn't say anything else. I needed my breath for running. I was glad when we finally got to Dana's house.

Dana was already home from school. She goes to Lincoln Elementary instead of Washington. It's only a few blocks away from her house. Dana was in the yard, bouncing up and down on her trampoline.

"Hi, guys," she called, in between bounces. "What's up?"

"We need to use your tramp," Katie said. "Amanda has to practice her vaults for the audition."

Dana stopped bouncing. "I have to practice, too," she said.

"But Amanda has the audition," Katie insisted.

"We'll *all* be working out when Mr. Sokolov comes," Dana said. "Maybe he'll notice how good the rest of us are."

"Please, Dana," I said. "You can use the tramp anytime. I only have two more days to become a perfect ten."

Dana hopped off the trampoline. "Oh, all right," she grumbled.

"Thanks, Dana," I said. "You're a good friend."

Dana *is* a good friend! But I could tell she was jealous. I didn't blame her. I would be jealous if *she* were the one auditioning for Jon Sokolov. Dana and I are the best gymnasts in our class. We've been rivals since my first day at Jody's Gym. It makes us both work harder.

That made me think — in Texas it would be strange not having Dana around to compete with in class.

"Amanda?" Katie said. "What are you waiting for? I thought you wanted to practice."

"I do," I said, climbing onto the trampoline.

"Let's start with some straddles," Katie said. "Then we'll work up to front flips."

"Okay." I jumped high in the air, lifting my legs in a vee. I put everything but straddles out of my mind.

"Again!" Katie shouted. "Keep your knees straight! Point your toes! And smile! Smile! Smile!"

It was hard *not* to smile. Katie is usually sort of shy. But today she sounded a lot like Coach Jody.

Katie made me do a million straddles. "All *riiight!*" she finally said. "Now let's see some handsprings."

I did a handspring. I kept my toes pointed perfectly. "Good going!" Katie

cheered. "Did you see that, Dana?" she asked.

But Dana didn't answer. She was sitting under a tree with Gabby. They weren't paying any attention to me.

I might as well be in Texas already, I thought. No one would even notice.

"Let's get back to work," I told Katie.

"I think you've practiced enough today," Katie said. Then she yelled to Dana, "Where's Woof? Can we play with her?"

Woof is Dana's dog. She's very cute — but not as cute as Zelda! Katie loves Woof anyway. She loves all animals.

"Come on, Katie," I said. "You can play with Woof later. First help me with my handstands." I set my hands on the grass and kicked up my legs. "Let's see how long I can hold this."

Katie waited while I counted the seconds out loud. I was up to 136 when Dana and Gabby walked over.

"Come down, Amanda," Katie said. "You'll hurt yourself."

"Come down before you fall down!" Dana joked. Gabby laughed.

"It isn't funny," I said, still upside down. "My whole Olympic career is at stake!"

All that talking threw my counting off, so I started again. This time I only got to nine before I wobbled and fell.

"*Now* will you stop?" Katie asked.

"Just one more," I said. I kicked up into another handstand.

Katie grabbed my foot. "Amanda!" she cried. "Your face is purple. You'd better rest now."

"Besides, it's almost dinnertime," Dana added.

"Well, I guess I should eat some dinner," I admitted. "To keep up my strength." I stood upright again. Dana's backyard swirled around me for a minute. "Wow, I

held that handstand so long that I'm dizzy!"
I said.

Nobody heard me. They were busy watching Gabby's leaf dance.

"Come on, Gab," I said. "Let's go. We'll be late for dinner."

"I'm staying *here* for dinner," Gabby announced.

"You're what?" I asked.

"I'm having dinner here!" Gabby repeated. "Dana said I could."

I looked at Dana. "You did? How come?"

"Gabby asked me to help her practice for the ballet recital," Dana explained.

"You?" I said. "I didn't know you took ballet."

"I don't anymore," Dana admitted. "But I used to."

"Dana is the best ballerina!" Gabby piped up. "You should see her dance!" She grabbed Dana's hands and they both went whirling around the yard.

"Well, if you're sure," I said doubtfully.

"Sure," Dana said over her shoulder.

"Sure," Gabby echoed.

"Great," I said. "Maybe now I'll be able to practice in peace."

"My mom will bring her home after we eat!" Dana called.

"Let's go pick up your bike on the way home," Katie said. She pedaled off down the street.

As I jogged after her, I felt kind of weird. I didn't have time to help Gabby with her ballet. But that didn't mean I wanted Dana to do it!

# 7

# The Return of Jon Sokolov

"Amanda, you look great," Katie said.

It was Thursday afternoon and I had just zipped up my new yellow leotard. I had raced home from school with Gabby. I didn't even go into the house with her. But now that I was at the gym, I didn't know what to do. I was so nervous that my hands shook.

"Want me to braid your hair for you?" Katie asked.

"Forget about her hair," Dana told

Katie. "Amanda needs to think about her bar routine."

"We can do both," I told my friends. I recited every step of my routine for Dana while Katie tugged at my hair.

I was describing my dismount when Katie tied a yellow ribbon around my braid. "Time to go," she said.

"Already?" I asked.

I could hardly breathe as we walked into the gym. I was so nervous! It was only 3:30 — Mr. Sokolov wasn't coming for another hour! How would I get through it?

Warm-up made me feel better, but it was over too quickly. After twenty minutes of running, jumping, and stretching, Coach Jody clapped her hands. "Enough warm-up. Let's get to work," she said.

We all gathered around her.

"Today we're going to concentrate on the bars," Coach Jody announced. "Amanda, why don't you go first?"

I peeked at the gym door before I mounted the bars. Maybe Coach Sokolov would come early. But there was no sign of him.

"Relax, Amanda!" Coach Jody called as I spun around the top bar. "You're stiff as a board. Loosen up!"

I tried to relax — but I couldn't. What if Jon Sokolov showed up in the middle of my routine? What if he was watching me right now? I knew I was doing a terrible job!

I flipped off the bottom bar for my dismount and made a wobbly landing. I took another look around the gym. Still no Mr. Sokolov.

"Amanda, what are you looking for?" Coach Jody asked.

"Nothing," I mumbled. Then I sat down on the mat.

"Okay. Hannah Rose," Coach Jody said. "Let's see what you can do."

Hannah Rose did pretty well — as usual. Next to me and Dana, she's the best gymnast on the team. Liz went next, then Emily, Dana, and Katie. Their routines all looked better than mine.

"It's almost time!" Katie whispered as she sat down near me.

"I am *so* nervous!" I whispered back. I looked at the clock on the wall. It was exactly 4:30. Where *was* he?

I brushed the chalk off my leotard. What if I mess up my audition? I thought. I might never get another chance like this!

But what if I *don't* mess up? Then I'll have to go live in Texas. I've never even been there! Do I really want to leave my friends? I wondered. My family? My coach? What about —

"Everyone to the practice beam," Coach Jody called. "Spot each other on cartwheels. I'll be right back."

Coach Jody hurried across the gym. I

wondered where she was going . . . and then I saw him!

Jon Sokolov stood in the doorway. He shook Coach Jody's hand. Then he waved at me!

It must be time for the audition, I thought. The other girls were already working on the practice beam. Katie flashed me a good-luck signal — fingers crossed. "Go for it, Amanda," Dana said.

Jon Sokolov and Coach Jody were talking in the doorway. Maybe they were talking about me!

I took a deep breath and marched over to them. "Hello, Mr. Sokolov," I said.

Coach Sokolov looked down at me. "Hello, young lady," he said. "Keeping your toes pointed?"

I nodded. "I've been practicing really hard."

"Glad to hear it," he said with a smile. "Keep up the good work." And without another word, he walked out of the gym!

I watched him go. I didn't know what to say. Or do. I just stood there, staring after him.

"Come on, Amanda," Coach Jody said. "Let's get back to work."

"B-but . . . where is he going?" I asked.

"Back to Texas, of course," Coach Jody said.

"Already?" I cried. Maybe he *had* been watching during class. Maybe he'd seen me mess up! I could feel tears filling my eyes. I tried to hold them back. "But what about my audition?"

Coach Jody looked confused. "What audition?" she asked.

"With Mr. Sokolov. He said he was coming back. To see me. Today. I–I'm supposed to audition for him," I tried to explain. "You were there last week when he said it. Don't you remember?"

Coach Jody put her arm around me.

"Oh, no," she said. "I think you misunderstood. Jon is an old friend of mine. He's been here all week for a training seminar, and now he's on his way home. He just stopped in to say good-bye."

"Oh," I murmured. Now I really felt like crying. I was so disappointed. And so embarrassed! Mr. Sokolov had never even *thought* of auditioning me.

"Amanda?" Coach Jody said. "Listen to me. You're a very talented gymnast. I'm sure Coach Sokolov would have loved to watch you perform. He just didn't have the time. Maybe when he comes back next year . . ."

Coach Jody squeezed my shoulder. She looked really sorry for me. That made me feel even worse. But before I could say another embarrassing word, Buddy ran over to us.

"Your mother's on the phone, Amanda," Buddy said.

Mom never calls me at the gym. I knew it must be an emergency. I ran down the hall to Coach Jody's office and picked up the phone. "Mom?" I said. "What's wrong?"

"Amanda — where's Gabby?" Mom demanded.

"Isn't she home?" I said. "I left her there after school. Just like I always do."

"Well, she isn't here now," Mom cried. "No one has seen her since school!"

"I'll be right home," I said. "I'll help you find her."

I raced back into the gym. "Katie! Dana!" I cried. "Do you know where Gabby is?"

They both shook their heads. "What's wrong?" Katie asked.

"She isn't home," I explained. "And my mom can't find her!"

"Practice is almost over," Coach Jody

said. "You'd better leave right now, Amanda."

"Thanks," I said. "Will you come, too?" I asked Dana and Katie. "Gabby's been hanging out a lot with you guys lately. Maybe she went to one of your houses."

"Sure," Katie agreed. "We'll go home and look!"

The three of us threw our jackets on over our leotards and ran for our bikes. I had been worried about the audition, but now I felt *really* scared!

My baby sister — missing!

# 8

# Where's Gabby?

The whole house was in an uproar when I got home. Everyone was looking for Gabby.

Gran was searching the attic. Gretchen was checking the upstairs closets. And Peter was on the phone, calling Gabby's school friends. Even Zelda was trying to help. She was out in the yard, sniffing around the bushes.

"Mandy! You're here," Mom said, hugging me tight. I could tell she'd been crying.

"Where's Daddy?" I asked.

"He's driving through the neighbor-hood in case Gab just wandered off," Mom said.

"What can *I* do?" I asked.

"Oh, Mandy, I don't know. Gabby looks up to you so much. She's always tagging after you. If anyone can find her, you can."

I didn't know what to say. I couldn't tell Mom that I'd been totally ignoring Gabby lately. I hadn't played with her. I hadn't listened to her. I hadn't helped her with her recital. All I'd done was think about myself and my stupid audition.

I didn't even know where to start looking.

"Don't worry, Mom," I said. "We'll find her."

Just then the phone rang. I raced to get it.

"Amanda?" Katie said. "Did you find Gabby?"

"No," I told her. "She isn't at your house?"

"Sorry," Katie replied. "I looked all over. My mom hasn't seen her, either. Maybe she's at Dana's."

"I hope so," I said. "Thanks, Katie." I hung up and called Dana.

Dana answered on the first ring. "Amanda!" she cried. "I was just about to call you."

"Did you find Gabby?" I asked. I twisted the phone cord nervously. Please say yes, I thought. Please say you found her.

"No," Dana said. "I was hoping you'd found her by now."

"Not yet." I said. "But I'll call you when we do."

I hung up quickly and ran to Gabby's room. "Gabby!" I called. "Where are you?"

My sister's stuffed animals sat lined up on her bed. I picked up Bubba the bear and hugged him.

Think! I told myself. Where would Gabby go? Why would she run away?

Suddenly I knew why. I remembered the time *I* ran away. Gretchen said I was too young to play with her and her friends, and I got mad. I decided to scare them, so I ran off and hid in my playhouse. Gabby was only four then. But she came and hid with me. She always wanted to be wherever I was.

"That's it!" I yelled.

I ran down the stairs. Mom was in the kitchen.

"Mom!" I said. "I think I know where she is."

"Where are you going?" Mom cried as I ran past her.

"To the basement," I replied.

"But we already looked there!" Mom said.

"Not where *I'm* going to look," I answered.

I raced down the steps to the basement. "Gabby?" I yelled. "Are you here?"

No answer. "Gabby?" I flicked on the dim light. The room was full of shadows. But then, in the back corner, behind a rusty bike and a pile of boxes, I saw it — my old playhouse!

I shoved the boxes aside and opened the playhouse door. Gabby sat curled up on the floor. Her face was streaked with tears.

I was so happy to see her, I almost started crying, too. I crawled into the playhouse and threw my arms around her. "Gabby!" I exclaimed. "Are you okay? What are you doing in here?"

"I was practicing," she said. "For when you go to Texas."

"Practicing?" I repeated. "Practicing what?"

"Practicing being alone — without

you," Gabby explained. "It's no fun." She burst into tears.

"Oh, Gabby," I said. "You're not going to be alone. I — "

"I tried to find a new big sister," Gabby went on. "Gretchen is a good sister, but she's too old to play with. I wanted someone just like you. I tried Katie and Dana. They're really nice. But they're not as much fun as you are."

I laughed and gave Gabby another big hug. "Don't worry," I said. "I'm not going anywhere. I'm staying right here."

"You are?" Even in the dark basement I could see Gabby's eyes light up. "Hurray!" she cheered, hugging me back.

"I can't move away," I said. "I'd miss you too much."

It was the truth. As I sat with my sister, I suddenly felt glad I wasn't moving to Texas. Really glad.

I was still a little embarrassed about my so-called audition. But it wasn't too bad. I didn't want to leave my family and friends, anyway.

I took Gabby's hand and pulled her to her feet. "Come on," I said. "Let's go tell everyone we found you!"

Mom and Dad were so happy to see Gabby that they didn't punish her for running away. Instead, we had a big celebration! Dad picked up four giant pizzas and three kinds of ice cream. The whole family gathered around the table — all seven of us.

When we finished the pizzas, Mom pulled out the ice cream. "Mandy, why don't you invite Katie and Dana over for dessert?" she asked. She looked at the ice cream cartons and laughed. "I think we have enough."

I had already called my friends and told them about Gabby's hideout — and my audition mix-up. Now I called them back and asked them over. A few minutes later there were nine people at our table!

When the last spoonful of ice cream was gone, Katie, Dana, and I went up to my bedroom. Gabby followed us.

"Are you upset about the audition?" Dana asked.

I shook my head. "I was at first," I admitted. "But not anymore."

"Good!" Dana said. "Because we're happy you're not moving to Texas."

"Yeah," Katie agreed. "You just got here! It would be terrible if you left so soon!"

I smiled. "I didn't really want to leave," I admitted. "But I'm happy you guys want me to stay."

"Are you *sure* you're not upset?" Dana asked again. "I think *I* would have been — just a teensy little bit."

"No," I insisted. "I'm not ready to

move away from home yet. And Coach Jody said I might get to audition next year!"

"That's great!" Dana said. "Then at least all the training you did won't be wasted."

I laughed. "It wasn't wasted," I said. "With all the practicing I've done, I'm way better than you two!"

"Oh, yeah?" Dana joked. "I dare you to a handstand contest — right here, right now."

We laughed and kicked up into sloppy handstands. Then Gabby came around and tickled us until we all fell down in a heap.

As I lay on the floor with my sister and my friends, I laughed even harder.

Home! I couldn't imagine anyplace else I'd rather be.

It was perfect!

# JUNIOR GYMNASTS

# Can two people like different things and still be best friends?

Dana and Becky have been best friends all their lives. They're so close they even celebrate their birthdays together! But this year, when Dana wants the party held at Coach Jody's gym and Becky wants it someplace else, their friendship really gets put to the test.

## Junior Gymnasts #4
## Dana's Best Friend
### by Teddy Slater

**Vaulting into a bookstore near you.**